VIKING WARRIORS

by Sheri Dillard

The Child's World®

Published by The Child's World®
1980 Lookout Drive • Mankato, MN 56003-1705
800-599-READ • www.childsworld.com

ACKNOWLEDGMENTS
The Child's World®: Mary Berendes, Publishing Director
Red Line Editorial: Editorial direction
The Design Lab: Design
Amnet: Production
Content Consultant: Scott A. Mellor, Department of
Scandinavian Studies, University of Wisconsin–Madison
Design elements: iStockphoto
Photographs ©: Blue Lantern Studio/Corbis, cover; North
Wind Picture Archives, 4, 20; Steven Wright/Shutterstock
Images, 7; William Gray/JAI/Corbis, 8; iStockphoto, 11, 21;
National Geographic Society/Corbis, 12; Alison Wright/
Corbis, 13; Anthony Devlin/AP Images, 15; Gerry
Embleton/North Wind Picture Archives, 16, 30 (bottom);
Werner Forman/Corbis, 17, 30 (top right); Stapleton
Collection/Corbis, 23; DK Images, 24; Ted Spiegel/Corbis,
26, 30 (top left); Public Domain, 28; Yongyut Kumsri/
Shutterstock Images, 29

ISBN 9781631437618
LCCN 2014945428

Printed in the United States of America
Mankato, MN
November, 2014
PA02246

ABOUT THE AUTHOR

*Sheri Dillard has written
many stories for children.
She is a preschool teacher
who lives in Atlanta,
Georgia, with her husband,
three sons, and a 100-pound
puppy named Captain.*

TABLE OF CONTENTS

A Viking leader prepares his warriors for a raid.

CHAPTER ONE

KING HARALD III

Harald Hardrada was **heir** to the throne in Norway, but his country was a dangerous place. His half brother was Norway's King Olaf. But there were others who wanted to take control of the country. There were many battles over who would be the next king. In 1030, at age 15, Harald Hardrada fought in a brutal civil war. He was badly injured. When King Olaf was killed, Harald Hardrada was forced to flee for his life. But he knew he would come back to Norway. Harald Hardrada wanted to be king.

Harald Hardrada was a brutal warrior. During his **exile**, he led raids and fought many battles. He and his warriors sought wealth and **plunder**. Not only was Harald Hardrada a tough fighter, he was also very smart. When he was unable to break through a castle's thick walls in Sicily, Italy, Harald Hardrada had an idea. He noticed little birds leaving the castle to gather twigs. He ordered his men to capture the birds. The men attached burning twigs to the birds' backs and set them free. The birds then flew back to their nests. The burning twigs caused the buildings' thatched roofs to catch on fire. The castle grounds burned. During the chaos, Harald Hardrada and his men captured the castle and took its treasures.

Over time, Harald Hardrada became known as a great warrior and a strong leader. His men were loyal to him. He became wealthy through raids. When Harald Hardrada returned to Norway in 1046, his nephew was king. He convinced his nephew to share the throne. They ruled Norway together. Within the year, Harald Hardrada's nephew died. Harald Hardrada was now King Harald III, the only king of Norway.

THE VIKING HOMELAND

The Vikings came from Scandinavia, which is made up of Norway, Denmark, and Sweden. There were many independent groups of warriors. But together they became known as Vikings. The term *Viking* might have come from a place called *Viken* in Norway.

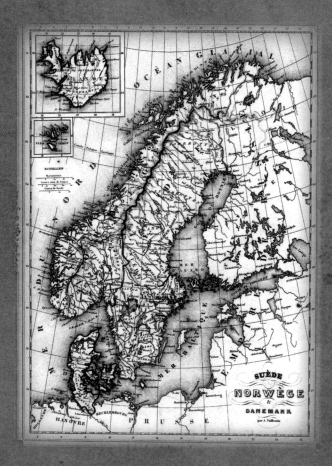

Scandinavia includes Norway, Denmark, and Sweden.

ANOTHER VIEW
A GOOD VIKING LEADER

To be a leader in Viking times, a man needed to be a good warrior. He had to show that he could lead men into battle and win. He also needed wealth to reward his followers. After a victory, the leader celebrated with a huge feast. Warriors were rewarded with good food, **mead**, wine, and treasure. Why do you think this made a leader's followers loyal?

Huge feasts took place in a Viking leader's house.

CHAPTER TWO

RISE OF THE VIKINGS

The Viking Age lasted from the late 700s through 1100. Before then, many Scandinavian people were farmers and raised cattle. They lived on large farms with their families. They struggled to survive in the land's tough conditions. The weather was brutally cold and the growing season was short.

In the late 700s, groups of raiders worked together and set out by sea to look for more land and plunder. They used their skills and tools to build wooden longships. These ships could travel in the open, rough seas. This allowed Vikings to travel to countries far from their homeland. The ships were fast. Each had a shallow **draft** and could be brought close to shore. The smaller ships could travel down rivers and were light enough to carry over land.

Early Viking raids happened in coastal areas of British Isles and Europe. Coastal towns were easy to get to and escape from. The raiders often attacked **monasteries** and churches. This made the Vikings unique and dangerous. Christians would not attack these holy places. The Vikings were not Christians, though. So they freely raided churches or places of worship. The Vikings stole treasure and the monks at the monasteries did not fight back.

One of the first known Viking raids was in 793 at a monastery in northern England at Lindisfarne. Soon, Vikings looked to larger cities in Europe. The continent's many rivers were perfect passages for the Viking ships.

The Vikings were not a large organized group with one leader. There were many Viking groups, each with a leader. Word spread about some of the strong leaders and skilled fighters. These men looked to gain power and land.

Vikings occasionally battled each other in their longships.

ANOTHER VIEW
RECORDING HISTORY

Monks and church officials recorded much of what is known about the Vikings. These people belonged to groups that suffered many Viking attacks. As victims, their viewpoints were one-sided. There are no writings of the events from a Viking point of view. How might a Viking tell the story of an attack on a monastery?

Viking invaders attack a monastery in Ireland.

THE VIKING LONGSHIP

The Viking longship was a useful boat for raids. It had a sail for ocean travel. The Vikings could also switch to oars to row the ship. Longships came in a variety of sizes. They could hold crews of 24 to 100 men. The ships were one of the Vikings' best weapons. They were fast, light, and easy to steer. Since longships could travel down rivers, the Vikings surprised many of their victims. They could attack, steal, and leave before any army could assemble in defense.

A longship is on display in the Viking Ship Museum in Oslo, Norway.

CHAPTER THREE

ARMOR AND WEAPONS

Vikings carried weapons for more than just fighting.
Weapons were also a sign of wealth and status. Many
weapons had gold, silver, and bronze decorations.
The most common weapons were swords, spears, and
battle-axes. Some warriors used bows and arrows and
other missile-type weapons, too.

Swords were difficult to make, and the best materials
were costly. Not many Viking warriors could afford
them. A good sword was light and strong. It also needed
to be flexible so it would not break if it became stuck in
an enemy's shield.

Vikings often used spears and short swords. A spear
had a metal blade atop a long wooden pole. Warriors
could throw two spears at once. Some warriors could

Viking swords and ax blades.

catch spears midair and throw them back at their
enemies. The short sword was typically 12 to 24 inches
(30 to 60 cm) long. It was carried in a sheath on a
warrior's belt for quick access.

Many men already owned axes for farming chores,
such as splitting wood. These axes could also be used in
fights. But battle-axes were typically lighter and easier
to use than farming axes. Some battle-axes had longer

Round shields and helmets protected Viking warriors.

handles, so two hands were needed to use them.
A warrior with this type of ax could not hold a shield.
He followed behind other Viking warriors and used
their shields for protection.

Most other warriors carried shields. The shield was
round and approximately 3 feet (1 m) wide. It was
made of wood and had a handle in the center. Shields
may have been covered in leather and decorated. Some
shields had a diamond shape.

Viking warriors wore heavy clothing and armor during battles. Mail armor was made of small metal rings connected together. It was made into a long shirt. Weapons could not easily pierce the metal rings. Mail armor was expensive and took a long time to make. The armor was heavy, weighing approximately 25 to 40 pounds (11 to 18 kg). Warriors had to be strong and fit to move around in the heavy armor. A belt was worn over the mail. It kept the entire weight of the armor from hanging on the warrior's shoulders.

This Viking helmet has an iron cap and a bronze crest.

Reindeer hide was also worn as armor. It was thick and effective padding. It absorbed blows from arrows and swords. Most leaders wore some kind of helmet, too. But unlike how they are often imagined today, the helmets did not have horns. They were typically made from several sheets of metal formed into a bowl shape. A nose guard was attached in front.

Bury the Sword

When a Viking warrior was killed, sometimes his enemies heated and bent his sword. The bent sword was then buried with the warrior. It was believed that this would decrease the power of the sword. The living warriors thought this protected them from the dead enemy warrior. If he sought revenge in the afterlife, he would not be able to use his bent sword.

Another View

EXPENSIVE PROTECTION

Being a prepared Viking warrior was expensive. Many warriors could not afford swords. Mail armor and helmets were costly as well. Mostly leaders wore these kinds of protection. How might a warrior with less protection than his fellow warriors feel when going into battle?

CHAPTER FOUR

BATTLE TACTICS

The Vikings were not an organized army of warriors. There was no single leader planning strategies and giving commands. Instead, there were many groups of Vikings. They acted independently, each group with a leader. It was important for a Viking leader to fight and win many battles. This helped him keep his followers loyal.

Longships were important for Viking battle tactics. Warriors brought their ships close to shore. They could attack quickly and then easily move on to the next unsuspecting town or monastery.

The Vikings started an attack by shooting arrows and throwing spears at the enemy. Sometimes, this

Viking raiders attack off the coast of the English Channel.

would be enough for a victory. If not, then the battle turned to brutal man-to-man combat.

The warriors approached the enemy in a single unit. The younger Vikings formed a line in front. They created a wall with their shields. The leader stood behind this wall with a bodyguard for protection. The older warriors supported from behind. The leader moved forward with his group. Sometimes, the warriors lined up in an arrow shape.

A group of Viking warriors enter and attack Paris, France.

As they got closer, the group rushed forward and tried to break through the enemy's defense. They wanted to capture or kill the enemy's leaders.

It was rare to have a battle on horseback. Sometimes, leaders rode horses to get to a battle quickly. But the fighting usually happened on foot. It was also rare to have a battle at sea. If there was a battle on water, it was usually close to shore. The Vikings connected their ships with ropes to form a line of ships. They shot arrows and other types of missiles at the enemy's ships. When the time was right, the warriors boarded the enemy's ships and fought man-to-man.

The Traveling Vikings

The Vikings traveled far from their homeland, unlike many other Europeans at the time. Their longships allowed them to travel across rough seas and down rivers. Some Vikings went to other countries to attack and plunder. Others traveled to start new lives as farmers, traders, or craftsmen. Vikings traveled west to England, Iceland, Greenland, and North America. They also made their way through Europe and as far east as Constantinople, which is in current-day Turkey.

Viking warriors battled the English in London in 1014.

ANOTHER VIEW
A VIKING CHILDHOOD

Viking children did not go to school. They learned about Viking religion, law, and history through songs and stories. They learned to hunt and use weapons. This later helped them as warriors. How might a young Viking child feel seeing his or her father or brother go off to battle?

A Viking family.

CHAPTER FIVE

FAMOUS VIKING BATTLES

In 793, Vikings attacked the monastery of Lindisfarne in northern England. This was one of the first Viking raids. The monks there did not expect the attack. At the time, it was not common for a Christian site to be targeted. The monastery was located on an island just off the coast. It was a quiet place where the monks could study and write. There were not many other people around. The monks were heading to worship when the Viking ships arrived. It was a quick and brutal attack. The Vikings took the monastery's gold, jewels, and other treasures. They killed the monks and burned the monastery.

According to legend, Ragnar Lodbrok led one of the first Viking river battles in 845. Lodbrok took a fleet of 120 ships and sailed down the Seine River to

A gravestone at Lindisfarne shows Viking raiders.

Paris, France. The King of France, Charles the Bald, was living in Paris. It was a well-defended city with an army, but the king did not want to fight. Instead, he gave the Vikings 7,000 pounds (3,175 kg) of silver so that they would leave.

Harald Hardrada led one of the last Viking raids in 1066. Tostig Godwinson, an earl and the brother of England's king, had visited him. Tostig Godwinson wanted help to overthrow his brother. Harald Hardrada imagined great wealth and a grand empire in addition to his kingdom in Norway. He loaded up 300 Viking ships and set sail. Harald Hardrada and his warriors attacked England's coast and made their way toward the city of York and the king. They plundered and set fire to towns. Many people had no choice but to become Harald Hardrada's followers. He continued on his path to York. He was certain that the king would surrender to him. Expecting no challenge, he did not bring all his warriors. But the king sent a huge army to fight Harald Hardrada. Rather than retreat, Harald Hardrada decided to stay and fight. Both sides lost many men. An arrow struck Harald Hardrada in the throat, and he died.

Harald Hardrada was a skilled warrior and a feared leader. He was the closest any Viking came to ruling a grand empire. But Harald Hardrada's final battle was a loss. Hardrada was Norway's king for 20 years. There were only a few more Viking raids and battles after that. The death of Harald Hardrada was the beginning of the end of the Viking Age.

Ragnar Lodbrok

Much of what is known about Ragnar Lodbrok comes from Icelandic **sagas**. Many were written 200 to 300 years after the events they describe happened. Some historians believe the stories of Ragnar Lodbrok are actually the stories of several men, including kings. Ragnar Lodbrok was a cunning warrior who made several successful attacks on France and England. He had a terrible death at the hands of Aella, King of Northumbria, England. Ragnar Lodbrok was thrown into a pit of snakes to die.

Ragnar Lodbrok's enemies left him in a pit of snakes.

ANOTHER VIEW
ICY GREENLAND

The Vikings were also explorers. Around 985, a Viking named Erik the Red was exiled from Iceland for killing his neighbors in a fight over land. He settled on a large island that was covered in snow and ice, but he found a small area where he could farm. When he returned to Iceland, he hoped to convince others to return with him. He called the new land Greenland. How might Viking people have felt when they finally arrived in Greenland to start new lives?

Greenland is covered with snow for much of the year.

TIMELINE

Late 700s

Groups of Viking raiders begin going on ocean voyages to look for land and treasure.

793

The Vikings attack the monastery at Lindisfarne.

845

Ragnar Lodbrok leads one of the first Viking river battles.

985

Erik the Red settles in Greenland.

1046

Harald Hardrada returns to Norway and becomes king.

1066

Harald Hardrada leads one of the final Viking battles and is killed.

GLOSSARY

draft (DRAFT) Draft is the distance between the waterline and the bottom of a boat when it is in the water. A longship has a shallow draft.

exile (EG-zile) To be in exile is to be in a time period of forced separation from one's homeland. Harald Hardrada lived in exile for many years.

heir (AIR) An heir is someone who will be or has been left money, property, or a title, such as king. Harald Hardrada was heir to the throne in Norway.

mead (MEED) Mead is an alcoholic drink made from honey and water. Viking leaders gave warriors food, wine, and mead at feasts.

monasteries (MON-uh-ster-eez) Monasteries are groups of buildings where monks live and work. Viking warriors often attacked monasteries.

plunder (PLUHN-dur) To plunder is to take something by robbery or theft. Viking men left their homeland seeking plunder.

sagas (SAH-guhz) Sagas are medieval stories telling the history and events of a family or culture. Icelandic sagas tell stories of Ragnar Lodbrok.

TO LEARN MORE

BOOKS

MacDonald, Fiona. *The Viking Codex: The Saga of Leif Eriksson*. East Sussex, UK: Book House, 2014.

Weintraub, Aileen. *Vikings: Raiders and Explorers*. New York: Children's Press, 2005.

WEB SITES

Visit our Web site for links about Viking warriors:

childsworld.com/links

Note to Parents, Teachers, and Librarians: We routinely verify our Web links to make sure they are safe and active sites. So encourage your readers to check them out!

INDEX